DRAKE HALBERD AND THE VEIL OF THE DEAD

a novel

D. J. KOWALENKO

iUniverse, Inc.
Bloomington

Drake Halberd and the Veil of the Dead

This is a work of fiction. All of the characters, names, incidents, organizations, and dialogue in this novel are either the products of the author's imagination or are used fictitiously.

iUniverse books may be ordered through booksellers or by contacting:

iUniverse
1663 Liberty Drive
Bloomington, IN 47403
www.iuniverse.com
1-800-Authors (1-800-288-4677)

Because of the dynamic nature of the Internet, any web addresses or links contained in this book may have changed since publication and may no longer be valid. The views expressed in this work are solely those of the author and do not necessarily reflect the views of the publisher, and the publisher hereby disclaims any responsibility for them.

Any people depicted in stock imagery provided by Thinkstock are models, and such images are being used for illustrative purposes only.

Certain stock imagery © Thinkstock.

ISBN: 978-1-4759-4796-0 (sc)
ISBN: 978-1-4759-4797-7 (e)

Library of Congress Control Number: 2012916340

Printed in the United States of America

iUniverse rev. date: 9/4/2012

Drake Halberd and the Veil of the Dead

CONTENTS

INTRO

The security guard clicked on his flashlight after the power went out. He walked down the hall and stopped when he heard strange banging, like someone pounding on a door. He turned around and went downstairs, to the basement. The door to the furnace room shook, like someone trapped down there was smashing on the door.

"Who's there?" the guard called. But there was no answer. He tried again, but there was once again no answer, just more banging. So he pulled out his keys and opened the door, keeping his flashlight and Taser with him.

"What the hell?" he grumbled in shock. Behind the door stood several grotesque, slightly rotting people, wearing mall uniforms and hissing. Foamy blood spewed from their deformed mouths. Their eyes were rolled back in their heads, and they stood with a crippled posture. He let out a blood-curdling scream as they lunged at him, biting and tearing at his body like flesh-hungry animals.

Chapter 1: Outbreak

The city streets were packed, the busy clusters of people all headed in different directions, making the poor traffic cop's job that much harder. Among those people stood a certain individual, wearing a khaki green short-sleeved shirt and blue jeans and putting on a brown leather jacket. Drake Halberd brought his hand through his black hair, scratching his head. He hadn't been to this city before, and he figured it was a good place for a vacation. *But vacations are supposed to be relaxing,* he thought as he wondered where to go. The wind blew, flinging some papers off of the street and smacking him in the face with a flyer, showing the new building complex project, Cosmic City. It was a massive building consisting of a multiplex cinema, apartment rooms, a shopping mall, and a hospital, among other things. It seemed like a decent place to spend his vacation.

When he arrived, it was just like he'd thought: the exterior was three times the size of every other building in the city, and it had a massive dome-like roof that made the place even more towering. By the mere size and shape alone, it looked like it cost millions of times more than any paycheque Drake had ever seen. And Drake was still on the outside. He opened the doors and then looked around. The place was large and roomy, but somehow it was still packed. There were plenty of sights, but the one that drew Drake the most right now, like a magnet, was the food court. There was every kind of food you could possibly eat. Drake had never seen a food court this big; fifty, maybe even sixty vendors covered the walls of the court, surrounding the hundreds of tables where people could sit and eat as they pleased. Of course, Drake had been around the world as a treasure hunter and had eaten a lot of the different types of food that was here, and he knew his favourites, but that didn't stop him from sampling other foods along the way. He hadn't eaten breakfast or lunch today, much unlike him, but it *was* a busy day. After Drake grabbed his food, he took a sharp look around and then pushed through the crowd of people to an empty seat. He then took a bite of his sub sandwich.

"Yeah, this is good," he said, pointing at it and then taking another bite. He then noticed something, someone he didn't want to find him. He packaged his sub and then jumped out of his chair and began darting through the crowd of people, pushing past them and attempting to escape.

"No, no, no. How? What happened? How was I found?" he mumbled, vaulting over a bench, nearly knocking over someone's drink. He then jumped on top of a blue recycling box, but before he could vault to the next floor, he was stopped by a voice.

"Hello, Drake," he heard from behind him, and he froze and then gave a half grin and turned around.

"Heh, heh, oh hey, Emma, what's g-going on with you?" he stuttered. His escape attempt hadn't worked. She brushed her golden brown hair from her shoulder and then huffed at him.

"You weren't trying to run now, were you?" she spoke in a hiss. Drake shrugged his shoulders, climbing off of the recycling box and avoiding her glare as if she were Medussa.

"Wh-what? Run? No, psh, no ... why would I run from you?" he said rather sarcastically. She made another huff and then spun away. She was then approached by a tall man wearing black. The man stroked his blond hair and then wrapped his arm around Emma's shoulder.

"What's up? Names Jacob," he introduced himself, not bothering to extend a hand for a handshake. Drake rolled his eyes. *Great, could it get worse?* Stuck between a snake and a "pretty boy," Drake smirked at himself. Karma. She had broken up with him because he was always putting their lives on the line. Then she got a new boyfriend who looked like he would be the first to flee at a problem. He tried to get a bite to eat and ended up with less than nothing. Karma was a bitch, 'cause it never worked.

It was then that another person arrived, wearing loose jeans, a jean jacket, and a grey T-shirt.

"Stuck in a hard spot, kid?" he said, grabbing their attention.

"Sullivan!" Drake called as the man walked up. Sullivan had been Drake's long-time friend and could easily spot when he was stuck in the middle of something uncomfortable.

"Hey, kid, you know, I have a great story about when I was in the mountains that would really—"

"Thanks, Sully, next time. Oh hey, look, I ... um, just remembered that I ..." Drake stuttered, looking for a way out of the situation. A scream then grabbed their attention. A figure dressed as Batman was robbing an old lady, running off with her purse.

3

"A robber … good timing," Drake announced, making a dash for the criminal.

Drake vaulted over the railing and ran across the long shopping mall's hallway.

"I thought Batman was a good guy?" Drake called, getting the robber's attention. The robber looked back and then tipped over a gumball machine in an attempt to slow Drake down. Drake swung his arms as he tried to keep his balance; then he jumped and continued the chase. Drake followed the robber through a corridor and into a large roomful of people dressed as superheroes and villains. Drake rolled his eyes—of course, it was Comic-Con, the world's gathering of comic book characters for a massive, crowded convention. He stopped for a breath and then pushed his way through a crowd. A few people brushed past him.

"Nice Nathan Drake costume," one of them complimented.

"Who is that?" Drake asked, shrugging his shoulders. He got no answer, so he continued his search. As he walked, Drake passed several different people dressed like Batman, but not one of them was the right one. He figured it would be easy to tell. Fat, small, and holding a purse. But after a while of pushing through the crowd, Drake was getting annoyed. Before he could make a remark about it, he noticed a door slowly closing as the purse carrying Batman slipped through it. So he ran for it and pushed through the large steel door and into the creepy back hallways. The hall was littered with crates and show props for the comic convention. It was filled with shelves of superhero toys, plushies, blow-up dolls, and many other stored items that would be used in the show or sold for profit at the vendors. Drake looked around and then followed the strange moaning sound. But this moaning wasn't of the "good" kind. As he walked, his foot kicked a flashlight on the ground. He bent down and picked it up. There was blood spattered on the ground and on the handle of the flashlight.

"Blood?" he wondered, placing his index finger under his chin. He was then spooked by a loud screeching noise. He followed the hallway and then saw four or five people all huddled around. He picked up the scent of rotting flesh and heard gross chewing and ripping sounds. Drake called, and the people turned, their faces covered in the dead Batman's blood. Their clothes were tattered, and bones stuck out of their sides. They all made a squealing noise and then charged at Drake. Drake's jaw dropped, and his eyes widened.

"Holy crap!" he said, and then he ran for the comic convention. He kicked through the doors and ran through the crowd, telling everyone to run. The creatures quickly followed, jumping on the people in the crowd and biting them hard. The people screamed and made a break for the door. Pushing and shoving, clawing their way out of the room. Drake was luckily the first one out.

Sullivan, who was still with Emma and Jacob in the centre food court where Drake had left them, looked up as a breaking news report came on.

"A deadly virus has broken out this morning at Cosmic City. 9-1-1 lines are being flooded with calls right now and are unavailable at this time. The massive building, Cosmic City, has been …"

"Sullivan!" Drake called, getting his attention. "We've gotta go! Now!" he yelled, taking deep breaths. Sullivan faced him and then quickly jumped out of the way of a zombie. The zombie continued charging forward and crashed through a store window landing on top of Emma. She screamed, trying to fight the creature off.

"Don't worry. I'll save you, Emma!" called her boyfriend. He grabbed on to a mop and smacked the creature off of her. She quickly got up and hid behind Jacob. The creature stood up and attacked Jacob, knocking him over. Jacob then screamed, begging for help. Drake grabbed the mop, smacked the zombie off, and then broke the end of the mop and rammed it through the zombie's head. The zombie wriggled for a few seconds and then died. Drake breathed heavily, tearing the mop out and dropping it on the ground. He then helped Jacob to his wobbling feet.

"Real heroic," Emma huffed at Jacob. Jacob patted himself down and then turned around.

"I had that," he responded. Drake shook his head, remembering Jacob's words:

Help, oh God, somebody help me! He knew he should've said something but left him with whatever was left of his pride, no matter how wet Jacob's pants were.

"Was that a zombie?" Drake asked Sullivan.

Sullivan looked. "I don't know, but for now let's just get to the exit. Come on!" he replied, jogging towards the exit.

Drake, Emma, and Jacob followed closely behind him. Amongst the crowd of panicking people, they saw the doors barred and covered in a thick metal sheet that could take an explosion. Everyone stopped in their tracks. The building was in lockdown. Zombies were real and attacking people. There was panic everywhere as people pounded on the doors, windows, and their cell phones. Sullivan looked up at the TV.

"Repeat: This is a recording. Due to an overwhelming amount of calls, 9-1-1 is currently inaccessible. An outbreak

is reported at the Cosmic City building, and the authorities have the building on lockdown to contain the virus. No new news can be reported at this time."

"Crap, this *is* bad," Sullivan said, covering his face with his hands.

"This cannot be happening," Drake mumbled, pacing. The building was locked down. A virus was spreading, there were zombies, and utter chaos everywhere. How could things get worse?

Chapter 2: Lockdown

Drake, Sullivan, Emma, and Jacob all crept through the theatre section of Cosmic City, searching for food. Jacob had argued that food could be better found in the *food* section of the shopping mall, but Drake had countered that remark by saying that that's the same thing everyone else would be doing, thus diminishing their chances of finding food. But the theatre has refrigerators that hold sandwiches and other goods, such as water bottles. So they ended up going that way. After all, no one knew more about finding food than Drake.

"Quiet, quiet," Drake whispered as they slipped by a pack of zombies that were chewing on a dead pedestrian, "we all have to be ... quiet," he continued saying, before stepping on a crunchy bag of potato chips. They all stopped walking as the dozen zombies all turned to face them.

Surrounded, Drake did the only thing he could think of at the time. "Run!" he screamed as the group made a dash towards the exit, smacking aside zombies and grabbing what they could along the way. The zombies swarmed them like hungry locusts, giving fast chase to their prey. As Drake ran, he tipped over some stands to block the advancing zombies, and it worked. The creatures tripped over the stands and each other trying to get to the four Happy Meals in front of them.

"The door, the door!" Jacob screamed, running at the exit. The four of them made it out and found themselves in the Fountain Plaza courtyard. It was mostly clear of people, aside from a couple of limping zombies and some people scrambling through a door at the other end of the courtyard. The group started to run again but were stopped by a noise on the large speakers that were placed around the plaza.

"This is Mason Remirev, of the SPU. If you're alive out there, anybody, come to the Government Survival Bunker as soon as you can. Remember, you're not alone."

"SPU ?" Drake asked. Emma sighed and poked her own forehead.

"Special Protection Unit, of the military," she replied. Drake looked at her and shrugged.

"Sounds like a good idea," Sullivan spoke up.

"How do we get to it?" Drake asked, and then he turned his head and saw a map of Cosmic City, with one room circled in red.

"Oh, that helps," he continued, taking the map off the wall and placing it in a pouch that was wrapped tightly around his leg. He stood up again and waved his hand, telling them all to follow him.

"Halfway there," Drake announced, turning the map from side to side.

"Are you reading that right?" Emma asked, taking the map.

"Yes, I'm pretty sure—" Drake began saying, but he was cut off by a crowd of crazed zombies charging them from behind. He opened his mouth to say something but was once again cut off by an arrow shooting past his head. He ducked and then turned around. A young girl wearing what looked to be a typical schoolgirl's outfit, stood behind them, holding a bow and stringing in a new arrow. She flipped her long dark brown hair out of her face and then took aim at another zombie.

"Oh yeah, sure, a schoolgirl with a bow. Who would have thought?" Drake said

"Sure hope she's on our side," Sullivan replied. The girl fired another arrow straight into a zombie's head.

"Well, let's go! Come on!" she called, leading them down a hallway to an elevator marked SPU.

Drake turned and tried to go back, only to be stopped by an identical-looking girl, holding a sheathed sword to his chest. "What is it?" she asked.

Drake looked around. "I need my chain," he replied, pointing to a chain lying on the ground with what looked like a ring attached to the end of it. The girl nodded and then turned around. She made a quick dash, beheading a few zombies along the way with her katana. She continued slashing until she made it to the chain. She passed it back to Drake, and then they all stepped into the elevator.

"And another girl using a sword. What is this, an anime?" Drake said quietly to himself.

"You still have that thing?" Sullivan asked as Drake put the chain around his neck. Drake nodded as the elevator doors opened. Inside, there stood monitors and plenty of bunk beds, along with a food storage shelf that contained enough food for a few days. A man approached the elevator, introducing himself.

"The name's Mason, Mason Remirev. Good to see you could make it."

"Yeah, we're glad too. So who are they?" Drake replied, gesturing towards the twins.

"This," Mason started, putting his hand on the one with the bow, "is Jayde. She's the head of her archery class. And this," he put his hand on the other girl, "is Angel. She's the kendo clubs best student. And they're *both* my little girls. So don't think of anything cute, you hear?"

Drake nodded quickly. Mason turned and raised his arms, showcasing the entire room. "And finally, this is the bunker. Not pretty, but it'll last."

Drake then had the look of someone who had an idea. He searched his bag and pulled out his sandwich, taking another bite of it. He then spotted a young boy sitting in the corner and looking hungry. Drake stared sympathetically at the boy, remembering a time when he was seven years old.

***

Drake, at age seven, raced across a rooftop and jumped over some boards. He was in a city where the buildings were sandstone coloured, the roofs made of weak wooden boards. He was being chased by the town guards for stealing food. Every day was a fight for him. Food, water—hell, even a place to sleep. All of the bare bone basics a human needed to survive he had to fight for.

Drake jumped across to another roof. Then the boards broke, sending him falling into the building. Drake, vision hazy, looked up to see what looked like a thirty-year-old man, standing before him, smiling.

"Who-who are you?" he asked the man.

"The name's Sullivan. You look like you're in trouble. Need some help there, kid?" the man replied, extending a hand.

***

Drake shook his head and then walked over to the hungry kid and broke his sandwich apart, handing half of it to him. The kid smiled and took a bite of the sandwich enjoying the food he was given. Drake then walked over to the other end of the bunker, where Sullivan was.

"You know, he was probably just scamming you?" Sullivan told Drake.

Drake shook his head. "Who cares? That's what I would've done," he replied.

Sullivan smiled and shook his head.

"Hey, look at this!" called Mason, and everyone came running over to the monitors. A teenager stood at the other end of the camera, still playing arcade games in the game room.

"What is he doing?" Drake asked, watching the monitor, noticing some shambling shadows behind the plump orange-haired kid. "I'll go get him!" he continued, turning towards the door. Mason placed his hand on Drake's shoulder, stopping him.

"I can't let you go out there!" he said, and Drake smirked.

"It's fine … I'll just go get him and be back, swear!"

Mason moved his hand away from Drake's shoulder, nodded, and then replied, "All right, but I have to keep the elevator down here to keep the zombies from piling in!" Drake nodded to that and then picked up a walkie-talkie before going on his way. Jacob stopped Drake just before the elevator, telling him not to screw up, and then handed him a broken stick for defense. Drake smirked slightly, thinking that the gesture was nice but that it really wouldn't help much. He then continued towards the arcade in Cosmic City's entertainment room.

When Drake arrived he called to the plump teenager. The teen turned around and his blood shot eyes grew wider than a cow, creeping Drake out to no end.

"We, uh, we've got to go. A safehouse is just this way," Drake explained.

"*No*! No, I'm not done yet! Do you have quarters for me?" the teen replied.

"No, but what's your name? Come on we've gotta go!" Drake answered, extending a cautious hand. The kid didn't seem quite right.

"My name is Billy. But I'm not going yet! You want to take me away from games! Just like my mom and dad did, and now they're dead!"

That statement gave Drake the chills. Had Billy killed his parents? For arcade games? Something was wrong, very wrong. Billy's eyes grew wider as he pulled out a hand gun.

"Time for a boss battle!" Billy screeched, firing at Drake. Drake ducked and rolled, jumping behind one of the arcade machines. As he did, a bullet whizzed by his arm, cutting him.

Damn!" Drake cursed, squeezing his arm.

"One hundred points! Come on out, my target!" Billy chuckled.

"A hundred points?" Drake grumbled, peeking around the corner. He hid again as Billy fired another shot. Drake looked around and then grabbed on to a tray of food, tossing it at Billy. Billy shook his head and shot again. Drake slid towards another machine and then got an idea.

"You're running out of lives! Looks like its game over for you! Time to restart!" Billy screamed as he walked around the corner. Billy's mind had probably been breaking all his life, and the sudden outbreak of crazed zombies must have pushed him over the edge. At least that's what Drake thought. Drake stood up and bashed Billy in the chest with a small table, sending him staggering back and tripping over some railings. Billy wriggled a bit, and an arcade machine began tipping. Drake noticed and made a dash for Billy. But he was too late, as the machine fell on Billy's head, killing him. Drake slammed his hand on the machine and took some deep breaths. The kid was psycho, but didn't deserve to be killed by his favourite game machine! Drake then stood up, taking Billy's hand gun and sprinting off towards the bunker.

It then dawned on Drake that if Billy was out there, there were other survivors, and maybe he could actually save them...

CHAPTER 3: SURVIVORS

Drake jumped, landing on a magazine kiosk, flailing his arms trying to regain his balance. He breathed deeply and then looked around. He was surrounded by zombies, with nothing left to jump to. He then turned to his left and saw a golf cart driving up to the kiosk, running down a few zombies along the way.

Sullivan, Emma, and Jacob.

Sullivan reached into his pocket and drew the revolver that he always carried around and began firing it, killing more of the zombies in their path. The gun was a six-shooter, so Sullivan had to be careful to make each shot count.

Drake smiled.

"Sullivan!" Bout time you showed up here!" he called as the cart pulled up, letting Drake jump onto the roof. Drake's walkie-talkie then buzzed. It was Mason.

"Hey kid, you should go check out the sub trains. Something fishy is going on."

Drake shook his head.

"This building has its own train?" he exclaimed, looking down at the other three. Emma nodded. Drake frowned and shook his head. *Maybe I should've checked the maps before*

I entered the food court, he thought, pulling out his map and giving directions to Sullivan as he sped down the main corridor of the mall.

The golf kart finally pulled up beside the tracks, and Drake saw two passenger cars moving side by side down the tracks.

"Speed up, Sullivan! Hit the pedal to the metal!" Drake called down. Sullivan pushed on the pedal hard, hitting the maximum speed for the golf kart just moments later. Drake raised an eyebrow and then shook his head. It would have to do. Drake crouched and then jumped off of the kart and onto the side of the passenger car, clinging onto the hand railings. He struggled for a bit, and he was barely able to pull himself into the train and avoid the sign that flew by. Drake balanced himself out and then looked around. No one.

So he checked the other passenger car. A man came walking out from the shadows of the other train, clapping his hands.

African American, about six feet tall, and wearing some sort of short-sleeved tuxedo.

"Jax Caupo," he introduced himself. "You did good finding me, Drake Halberd."

"Umm, who are you again?" Drake asked, a confused expression on his face.

"The one who began this … madness … the zombies." They're quite the creatures, you know? Fast and brutal in groups … but weak when they are alone," Jax replied in a sinister manner, pulling out a 12-gauge shot gun, "like a family."

Drake dropped to the ground, rolling away from Jax's blast. Drake pulled out the hand gun that he had gotten from Billy and fired back, with Jax taking cover.

"I'm not alone you know? There is another. But by the time you find out who that is, it will be too late, Drake Halberd!" Jax screamed, shooting his gun at Drake. Drake rolled again, avoiding the shotgun's blast as it ripped through the wall of the train.

"Look out Drake!" Drake heard Emma scream on his walkie-talkie. He looked and saw the tracks coming to an end. Drake then turned and ran for the far end of the passenger car. Everything seemed to slow as he approached the end of the train. He jumped just as the train shot off the edge of the tracks and plummeted fifty feet below. Drake managed to catch the very edge of the train track to hold himself up. He then turned his head and looked through the doorless back of the other train as it fell.

Jax, who was still in the other train, smirked at Drake and raised his middle finger, before the train hit the bottom and blew up. Drake turned his head to avoid the light of the blast. He then tried to pull himself up, but the tracks broke. Drake swung his arm and was caught by Sullivan.

"That's twice in a row kid. You owe me," Sullivan said with a grin as he pulled Drake up and onto the ground. Drake rolled away from the edge, panting heavily.

"Ugh, thanks, Sullivan. I owe you big time!" Drake breathed, getting back up to his feet.

Emma then screamed and the three turned in her direction, seeing an advancing wave of zombies. The four jumped into the golf kart, but it wouldn't start. Sullivan cursed and kicked the kart; then he climbed out and fired his six shooter at the zombies. The group ran south, but Jacob was caught by a small group of zombies and bitten several times. Emma screamed for him and tried to run back to him. Drake grabbed her arm and proceeded to drag her away, telling her that he was gone.

Drake knew that the zombie virus had infected him already. After all, the bite was the only way to transmit the virus. If it was in the air, water, or food, they would have it already and be zombies, not to mention everyone else who was bit had turned. Drake, after handing the crying Emma to Sullivan, turned around and shot Jacob in the head, mercy killing him and preventing his rebirth as a zombie. After a bit of a fight against the oncoming zombies, it began to look grim for the three survivors. A zombie lunged at Drake, but it was killed by an arrow shooting through the back of its head. The three looked and saw the twins backing them up. Angel drew her sword and cleaved through a swath of zombies, clearing the way for the group to escape.

After another while of walking, they made it back to the elevator and re-entered the safe house bunker. Drake sat down, breathing hard.

"I thought we were done. Man, I've gotta stop owing people," Drake said, hanging his head. Sullivan helped the sobbing Emma walk, sitting her on a chair and letting her mourn.

"Hey, glad you guys made it back. I'm sorry for Jacob, though. He was a good kid," Mason said sympathetically. Drake then looked over to the sobbing Emma. He felt bad for her. Sure, he didn't like Jacob much, but he *was* her boyfriend, and he didn't deserve to die like that. Drake shook his head and walked over to her.

"So, Emma—" he began to say before being slapped in the face.

"You're a bastard, you know? Every time I'm around you, bad things seem to happen," Emma cried out, smashing her fists into his chest over and over. Drake caught her hands and hugged her as she cried. Drake's attention was then pulled towards Mason.

"Hey, guess what. The military has arrived! They're coming to pick up survivors!" Mason called as Sullivan, Angel, and Jayde came running up.

Drake looked at Sullivan, gesturing with his head for Sullivan to take his place. Sullivan grinned and shook his head.

"Get over here now!" Drake mouthed and Sullivan reluctantly walked over, taking Drake's place and holding Emma. Drake walked over to the monitors, looked, and then rubbed his chin. After a while of thinking, he turned and walked across the bunker, to the storage area. Everyone watched him curiously, waiting to hear what he had to say. Drake then turned around with a sandwich in his hands and took a big bite. Everyone's expression went from curious and hopeful to disappointed and depressed.

"What? Gotta eat if I'm going to check that out," Drake reasoned, taking another bite before packaging it up. He then shoved it in his pouch and jogged off towards the elevator.

Drake arrived near where the soldiers were coming in. He was, however, three floors up and watching them from a balcony view. He couldn't see much, so he pulled out his binoculars. He saw several heavily armed soldiers walk in, armed to the teeth with heavy assault rifles and full body armor. Drake's attention was then drawn towards a group of survivors running up to the soldiers.

The soldiers looked at them. "Project Burn Out. Consider them infected," said the one on the left. The soldiers then aimed their machine guns at the people and opened fire, massacring the whole group. Except one, who tried to run. The soldier tried to shoot, but his gun was pushed down by a heavily muscled man wearing camo. He sported a stereotypical military buzz cut with grey hair and a mustache. He smirked and pointed a high-caliber hand gun at the fleeing person, shooting him in the head. The military group then continued moving in, being followed by several more platoons and an Armored Personal Carrier, or APC.

Drake was left stunned. He could feel the heat draining from his complexion.

Project Burn Out. Kill everything in the building—dead, alive, or otherwise. Drake put away his binoculars and headed back for the safe house. "How could things get any worse?"

CHAPTER 4: BURN OUT

The soldiers advanced through the mall quickly, shooting down everything that got in their way. Drake managed to sneak around the higher floors without being detected, doing his best to both gather intel and race the military towards the safety bunker. As he watched the military, it looked as though this wasn't their first time dealing with zombies.

Drake continued back to the bunker. He knew that if Mason, one of the SPU, and part of the military knew about it, then so would the soldiers. And so he had to get there as fast as possible. That was where Drake got his idea. Above him, there were catwalks. Small sections lead all over the mall like a closely knit network. It was there that he could take as many short cuts as possible. And so, Drake climbed the nearest support column and vaulted over the catwalk's safety rails. He then turned around, looking at the doors in front of and behind him.

"Well, this was a good plan. Now where the hell do I go?" Drake mumbled, deciding on the door in front of him. Drake was then forced to the ground by a massive explosion. It blew apart the walkways to the left of him. He stood up and looked. An assault helicopter, armed with mini-guns and rocket launchers, came flying through the new hole it had made in the wall. Drake ran towards the door ahead of him, screaming, "Oh crap!"

The chopper noticed him and started firing its mini guns. Drake slammed through the door and the helicopter fired two missiles, blowing down the door and slanting the walkway. Drake stumbled but recovered fast enough to avoid the mini-gun onslaught.

"Project Burn Out requires a helicopter?" Drake screamed, jumping across a gap in the walkways. The helicopter then fired more missiles, destroying Drake's only way out. He was now stranded on one piece of crumbling walkway. The helicopter flew over him to reacquire him as a target. As it did, Drake turned around and made a run for the helicopter, jumping as far as he could and grabbing on to the chopper's landing gear.

"Where the hell is he?" Drake heard the pilot ask in a panicked voice as he was flung around by the turning helicopter.

Drake cursed as he crawled up and banged on the window of the helicopter. The pilot turned and saw Drake pulling out a handgun. Drake tried to shoot, but the pilot spun the chopper to try and shake him off. The tail of the helicopter smashed against a wall and the chopper began to spin out of control. Drake screamed as he leapt from the chopper onto the nearby catwalk, with the chopper's blades slashing his pant leg before crashing down below and exploding, taking out the entire Yutan Casino. Drake panted heavily as he pulled himself up.

"Now where do I … oh, that's convenient," Drake said as he noticed a sign that read, "Security room ahead." Drake stood up and checked for his handgun, but it was gone. He shook his head and walked through the broken steel door and into the security room. Monitors, and lots of them, connected a massive main frame that controlled one third of the security in the building. Drake looked around and saw something strange. A dead person sitting on the office chair in front of the security monitors. But no zombie had killed this person. Drake turned the man's head and saw a bullet hole between his eyes. It looked as though the shot had come from a high-caliber handgun. Drake stood up and checked the monitors. The safe house had been breached. Soldiers lead Emma, Sullivan, Mason, and the twins out of the bunker and packed them into the APC. Drake narrowed his eyes. Why would they take prisoners? They had gunned down those survivors earlier, so what gives? Drake then zoomed in and saw the general talking with someone who was out of focus. The two then boarded the APC and drove off. Drake began to feel a knot in his stomach as he sat back in the chair, worrying about the fate of his friends. Drake then leaned forward, watching the APC head towards what looked like a small encampment of soldiers. His friends were then kicked out and led towards a tent. Drake shook his head, and suddenly he heard a squeal. He was pushed to the ground by a snarling zombie. The zombie bit at Drake, just missing the tip of his nose. Drake struggled, almost getting bit again, until he finally grabbed on to the dead security guard's pocketknife and rammed it through the zombie's head, killing it. Drake threw the corpse off of himself and quickly got up. He then dusted himself off and looked around.

"Heh, good thing nobody saw that," he commented, smirking to himself. Suddenly a cluster of zombies burst through a door, forcing Drake to escape through another door. Drake darted across the walkway, running as fast as he could, but he still felt the breath of the zombies on his neck. He leapt over the guard rail, grabbing the extension ladder, narrowly escaping the zombies.

Drake continued working his way across the mall, finally arriving near the military base. He snuck as close as he could to the encampment, pulling out his binoculars. Drake started with the food tent and spotted a guard taking things into his own hands. He was having Emma cook for him, wearing nothing but an apron. Drake raised an eyebrow.

"Why didn't I think of that?" Drake asked himself before shaking his head and smirking at the thought. He continued scouting, finding Sullivan and the twins being led into Cosmic City's jail room. But he couldn't find Mason anywhere. Drake shrugged and put away his binoculars. He crouched down and hid behind a crate at the edge of the camp. After peeking around the corner, Drake made a run for a tent, grabbing on to and knocking out a guard. Drake then quietly entered the food tent, creeping up and grabbing the guard who was leaning back and enjoying the show, smashing him on the back of the neck with his forearm and knocking him out cold. Drake then stopped, staring at Emma. He shook his head and tapped Emma's shoulder. She jumped and turned around.

"Where the hell were you? What took you …? This guy's been … been …" she yelled, pointing at the now out cold guard. Drake smirked and took off his tattered brown leather jacket, wrapping it around her. Drake then leaned down and picked up the guards machine gun and pistol. Drake walked out of the tent, telling Emma to stay put. She huffed at him and folded her arms across her chest, slowly backing up and into the tent.

Drake shook his head and then ran across to a different tent. A soldier noticed him and approached where he thought Drake had gone. Drake popped out and smacked the guard on the back of the neck, knocking him out. Drake dragged the body out of sight and then headed through the camp and to the cell blocks where Sullivan and the twins were being held. Drake jumped down and smacked a guard on the back of his head and then strangled him until the guard passed out. He breathed deeply and grabbed on to the guards keys. Drake attempted to open the doors, but was bashed over the head by a soldier. Drake rolled onto his back and crawled back a bit as the soldier pointed his machine gun at Drake's head. Drake shielded his face with his arms and then heard a smack. He looked up just in time to see Emma bash the soldier in the face with a frying pan. She looked down at Drake, leaning on her hips a bit and smirking as she raised an eyebrow. Drake knew that look too well. "Yeah, you were wrong," it said. Drake shook his head and took her hand as she helped him to his feet. Drake rubbed the back of his head, opening the cell doors.

"Drake, 'bout time your dead ass got here!" greeted Sullivan, as he hugged Drake. The twins said their thanks before ransacking the guard for weapons. Angel took the bowie knife while Jayde nabbed his AK-47.

The doors then blew down as a dozen soldiers rushed the gang. Drake jumped behind a steel crate and opened fire. Their cover was blown. Jayde jumped behind a wall and fired at the two soldiers on the far right, killing them. Angel continued searching the body, until she found what she was looking for. She smirked and walked past the shooting Sullivan, unpinning and throwing the frag grenade. The soldiers scattered quickly, but not fast enough to avoid the explosion. The group then dashed out the door, avoiding some gunfire. It was then that a golf kart equipped with steel sheets on the sides pulled up.

"Jump in!" Mason screamed while shooting. The group jumped in and the kart sped off. Drake breathed deeply and then asked Mason where he had been.

"I was escaping! Nice timing, by the way!" Mason called back. Sullivan opened his mouth to speak, but before he could begin, a wall was blasted down. The six people looked to see yet another attack helicopter.

"No, not you again!" Drake yelled, firing his gun at it. The chopper fired two rockets, which exploded beside the kart, throwing it off balance. The kart slid around and tipped on a sink hole in the middle of the mall, the same hole where the trains had fallen earlier. Drake fell out of the kart, just barely grabbing the edge of the sink hole. He cursed and his grip broke. Sullivan reached out, swinging his hand. The tips of their fingers touched, but Sullivan missed and he watched as Drake fell into the deep dark hole, screaming, "Holy crap!"

Honestly, how could things get any worse for Drake?

CHAPTER 5: TUNNELS

Drake awakened deep down in the crater, with his head throbbing in pain. As he sat up, he realized that his fall had been broken by the safety railings on the back of one of the train cars. Drake moaned as he got up. It was extremely dark, with only a little light shining from above to light up the place.

Where was he?

Drake shook his head and then stood up and moaned, falling to his knees and clutching his side in pain. The fall was harder on him than he had first thought, but there were no evident signs of serious injury or broken bones. But the sharp pain in his side might have suggested otherwise.

"Yeah, that makes it easier," Drake said sarcastically, as he pulled himself to his feet. Drake pulled out his flashlight and clicked it on. He then realized that he was in some kind of deep tunnel system, like an underground railway for trains, or miners. Could OnLast, the company who designed and built Cosmic City, have been trying to cover this up? But why, what would be so important that it needed to be covered up by such a big mall? Drake looked down at his feet and saw some kind of green gem. Emerald? The questions continued swirling through Drake's mind as he wondered why covering up a mine of Emeralds would benefit OnLast? Drake picked up the gem and pocketed it and then limped his way through the train car, arriving at the mouth of the destroyed cave. Drake then dropped to his knees, avoiding the swarm of bats that rushed him from the dark tunnel. Drake ruffled his hair and then stood up and continued going through the tunnels. As he walked, he heard a clicking noise. Drake stopped and then looked towards his flashlight. It was dying.

"Oh, come on!" He cursed as his flash light went out. He then pocketed it and continued walking for a while longer, until his path slowly became illuminated by a strange green glow. He looked up to see more emeralds sticking from the wall, glowing ever so slightly, just enough to light the way. Drake pulled out his green stone and saw that it was doing the same. Emeralds didn't glow in the dark. Drake's first thought was radioactivity. If that was the case, Drake was already screwed. He pocketed the gem and continued walking, hoping he wasn't right. Then again, according to Emma, Drake was never right, so maybe he was in luck? But Drake knew his luck—just when he hoped he would be wrong, he would be right. Drake let those thoughts trail to the back of his mind and continued walking through the glowing tunnel.

Drake finally came across a clearing, only to find some zombies crawling around on the walls of the cave. Drake ducked below a large rock in front of him. He slowly lifted his head over the rock. Just as he did, a zombie noticed him. It opened its mouth, which split into three parts, two on each side of its face and one on the bottom, each with a set of jagged, broken teeth. It hissed at him, calling to the others that he was there. It then spat a gob of green vomit at Drake. Drake ducked as the gob hit the boulder, melting through it.

"Of course, acid-spitting zombies. Why not?" Drake said hysterically as he jumped over the melting boulder and ran across the thin path of rock that clung to the edge of the wall. Drake ran as the path started melting under his feet. One of the spitters got smart, and spat at the ground ahead of Drake. Drake cursed and jumped, landing on a falling piece of pathway. He held tight and jumped, grabbing on to the stones sticking from the wall. Drake tried to pull himself up, but the stones came loose, and he went plummeting into the underground pond below. Drake struggled to get his bearings in the dark pond. It then began to get light again. More green glowing rocks. Drake stared for a second and then swam up to the surface of the water, catching his breath. He then looked over to see dead spitters falling into the water.

"It's about time, Sullivan!" Drake said happily, swimming over to the low edge of the pond. What he saw wasn't his friend, but rather heavily armed men in what looked like futuristic battle suits ripped right out of science fiction, bearing the name OnLast engraved on their shoulders. They reached in the water, yanked Drake out, and handcuffed him. "Come on!" Drake groaned.

"Let's get moving," said one of the men. Drake could tell that his voice had been heavily augmented by a computer installed in his helmet. The other nodded and the two men dragged Drake off.

***

Sullivan shot at the still pursuing helicopter with his AK-47, blasting at the pilot with all he had while Mason swerved around the copter's bullets, racing through the shopping centre of Cosmic Cities mall sector. Emma just sat in her seat stunned, Jacob was dead and now Drake was gone. He was most likely dead too. This was her worst trip ever.

Mason swerved as hard as he could without flipping the kart, avoiding the missiles that the copter fired. Mason then headed straight for the trains subway tunnel. It was too late for the helicopter to pull away and it smashed into the wall, blowing through it and exploding, almost collapsing the bridge on top of the kart. "Cut that one close, Mason!" Sullivan cursed, smiling. Mason grinned back.

"Nothing better than close," he replied.

***

"Ain't it beautiful?" asked Jax, as he paced back and forth in front of Drake, who was tied securely to a chair. Drake shook his head, waking himself up. Drake looked around, he was in some kind of dome shaped room, likely still underground somewhere in the tunnels. There was an elevator shaft in the room as well, but the elevator looked as though it had long since been removed. It was replaced by an electrical pulley that was used to lift heavy crates of emerald. Drake looked and realized that Jax pacing. But how? He was dead. He fell in the train car that exploded. "How are you alive?" Drake demanded, leaning forward confrontationally. Jax smiled, drinking green ooze from a vial.

"It's the secret, Draky baby, the one of immortality," Jax responded, staring at Drake with a sinister grin." See," he continued, "not everyone has the same luck that you do, Drake. So we need to improvise a bit. This right here is the key." Drake shook his head in disbelief. Jax had obviously lost it. Jax saw the disbelief and decided to prove his secret of immortality to Drake. "Need proof, Drake? Well fine then," he said as he walked over to a massive machine that was crunching the green stones that Drake had seen earlier. He stuck his hand in and Drake turned his head, hearing a scream of searing pain. He then just barely looked to see Jax's mangled hand, with blood spattering out of it. Drake almost threw up at the disgusting sight. Jax walked over and drank some more goo. And suddenly his hand began to quiver and shake. It unflattened and was perfectly healed.

"Ah, that's better! Don't you see, Draky baby? This is the beginning! The beginning of a revolution! I will become rich with my new invention!" Jax said as he laughed like a maniac. Drake gritted his teeth.

"You started this zombie overrun so that you could cover up your scheme, didn't you? Do you know how many people are dead?" Drake screamed.

Jax smirked at that remark. "What can I say? Sacrifices had to be made to better the world. You'll understand this one day, Drake."

Drake shook his head. Why did Jax keep talking to him like they knew each other? Maybe Jax knew Drake because he was a famous treasure hunter. Or was it just the way a psycho talked? Jax then turned and snapped his fingers. Drake glanced over just as a guard bashed him in the head with the blunt of his gun, knocking him out cold.

CHAPTER 6: ASCENSION

Drake awoke still tied to a chair, this time sitting in some kind of jail cell. But none of that was going to stop him now. He had to stop Jax, find some way to defeat the zombie infestation and escape with everyone's lives still intact.

His vacation had gone horribly wrong. Zombies were tearing people apart, and the military had moved in, killing everyone—alive or dead. Jax was planning on world domination with his eternal life stuff, and the rest of the group was still up on the surface with no safe place to bunker down. Drake dropped his head and slumped his shoulders. This was all in day one. Did his life suck that badly? Drake shook the negativity from his thoughts and then rocked side to side in his chair until he fell over on his side. As he did, he began to slip his hands out of the ropes he had been bound with. Years with Sullivan had at least taught him something important. A guard heard him fall over and walked up.

"What are you doing?" the guard boomed, opening the cellar door. He walked up and grabbed Drake by the hair, lifting him up. Drake smirked and brought his arms out from behind his back, surprising the guard. Drake took advantage, kneeing the guard away and wrapping the rope around the guard's neck, pulling him into the wall for a knockout. Drake knew the other guards would be coming quickly, so he grabbed the rifle leaning on the wall and then ran for the tunnel opposite to the one that he heard the noise coming from. He continued running until one of the bigger guards stopped him. He quickly lifted his rifle and began blasting at the guard's head, only to be fired back at, bullets nicking his arm as they whizzed by. But he managed to jump into cover before he was actually shot. The two battled for a couple more moments, until Drake had managed to avoid the guard's sight line long enough to climb on top of a large boulder at the centre of the tunnel. He then jumped down from above and smashed the guard over the head, knocking him out. Drake unpinned a grenade, chucked it down the tunnel, and then ran for his life. The tunnel blew, caving in and preventing his hostile followers from reaching him. Drake then arrived back at the centre room where the emerald grinding machine had been. He looked and saw Jax, holding on to the pulley cable, smirking.

"I knew you would escape, Drake. That's why I had this entire base lined with C4!" he said, laughing like a maniac. Drake looked around and saw bombs everywhere. He yelled as he ran as fast as he could go towards Jax. Jax released the lever, and the cable began pulling him up the elevator shaft. Drake pushed harder and jumped, catching Jax's leg just as he pushed the button. Explosions ripped through the building, loud booms and bangs. Drake held on, pulling himself up. Jax frowned and kicked Drake in the face, trying to make him let go.

"One-man ride, Drake!" he sneered at him. Drake swung, just avoiding a large light shaft almost splattering him. He found his balance again and began using Jax's clothes as leverage, pulling himself up and head butting Jax in the face. Fire raced up the shaft, threatening to engulf the two in flames. Jax punched Drake, who then punched back. The two duked it out until Drake bashed Jax's head into a light post that flew by, knocking him out. Drake then looked up and was flung out of the shaft, by the force of the explosion, blasting outwards like the fiery breath of a dragon. He rolled as he landed hard on the marble floor of the main hall. Drake moaned as he turned around and pulled himself up, holding on to his sore arm. Fire still filled the old elevator shaft.

"Well, look at that. I guess I didn't have to destroy that place after all," Drake said, shaking his head. He then turned around and walked over to Jax and began sifting through his pockets, pulling out a vile of green goo.

"I knew you had this on you," Drake said, pocketing the vile. Maybe the "immortal juice" had something to do with the zombie outbreak, but for now he had to find everyone else. Drake looked around and then headed south towards the Fishing World district.

***

Jax opened his weary eyes, the roof still tumbling around. He then looked a bit higher and saw a heavily built man with a buzz cut and wearing camo.

"You die, then come back again. You're just like them. I think we've outlived our little deal, Jax. Good-bye," the general said calmly to Jax, moving a high caliber rifle to point at Jax's head. He then squeezed the trigger, unloading an entire clip, before spitting and walking away.

***

Drake stopped walking, figuring he heard gunfire, but decided to continue onward. He just came from there, there was nobody there. He continued walking until he entered the Marinas District, which looked like a fish museum. The place ahead was flooded by some of the bigger fish tanks that had broken and swamped the entire place. Drake sighed as he pulled out his map. Yes, this was the only way back to the Central Mall Shopping District.

Drake prepped himself and then jumped into the water. He started swimming. Only moments later he heard a strange noise, like the noise of debris being clanked around underwater, and he turned to see what it had come from. What he saw wasn't a zombie, rather a shark pushing through the floating debris and attempting to eat him. Drake's eyes grew as he turned to swim faster, if only he'd done better at swimming classes. The shark reared behind Drake and opened its jaws, only to be smacked hard with a metal bat. Drake looked and then was pulled up out of the water by Angel and Jayde. The two had seen that Drake was about to be made into shark food and had jumped onto a piece of floating debris just in the nick of time to pull him up out of the water and bash the shark's face.

He coughed out water and then chuckled a bit.

"'Bout time you guys showed up," he said while trying to catch his breath

"Come on, we've gotta go!" called Mason as he fended off the zombies. The three jumped into the kart and Mason floored the gas pedal.

"Where are we going?" Drake asked, looking at Mason.

"I have no idea, kid," replied Mason as they sped down the district.

CHAPTER 7: THE CURE

Drake stared at the green goo, knowing that time was running out. There were still some survivors out there. And the military's Operation Burn Out was still in motion. Each person Drake had run into was looking for their own version of the cure for the zombie virus. Jax's goo, the military's Burn Out, and now he too was searching. Drake never thought, though, that the military would bring in helicopters. Things were getting chaotic, and he had to get to the bottom of things, but first he would need to deal with, or at least slow down, the military's plans. Drake stood up and placed the goo in the safety vault of the coffee shop they had been staying in as a makeshift bunker ever since their home base had been raided, taking the key with him.

"Where are you going?" asked Emma, walking up to him. Drake's expression was unwavering as he looked back and said,

"I'm going to shut down Operation Burn Out. They're causing problems."

Emma looked shocked. Drake was always into adventure, getting stuck in crappy situations, looking for rare old treasures, but he'd never purposefully gone toe to thousands of toes with the military. Had the zombies finally gotten to him? But she had seen the look in his eyes. He *was* serious, and there was nothing she could do to stop him now. Drake moved her aside and moved towards the exit of the coffee shop.

"Good luck, son," Mason said, nodding. Drake smirked and then continued on his way. Drake boarded the kart, which had been newly outfitted with scraps of sheet metal and steel floor grates as make shift armor, and sped off towards the military encampment.

It didn't take him long to arrive, but he had to park the kart back a ways to avoid detection. Stealth would be difficult due to the zombies, but if he stayed high, he could avoid most of them. Drake went prone and pulled out his binoculars. The base was heavily armed and there were guards everywhere. Each guard was on edge from the zombie's constant attacks. Drake knew what he had to do; it was easy enough to make a homemade bomb, for him, anyway. Drake rolled away and gathered supplies from nearby kiosks and booths, taking out the sentries stationed in the guard towers and stealing supplies along the way. Drake fixed six bombs and went prone, crawling under the jeeps and ATVs, setting and priming the bombs to detonate in two minutes. He then quickly escaped the area. Drake grinned, counting down in his head, until finally, *boom.* The entire stockpile of vehicles exploded, throwing twisted metal and shrapnel everywhere. The base flew into high alert, and everyone swarmed the dead vehicles like an angry ant nest. The noise also alerted all nearby zombies, causing every zombie in the area to stumble towards the military encampment. Drake noticed that zombies seemed to be attracted to noise. Probably as a way to find people. Drake never thought his plan would work so well. He jumped down and ran, ducking down and stealing his way through the chaos, priming two more bombs by ammunition stockpiles, taking what he needed first. He then turned around and stood face to face with several guards. Drake lifted his arms quickly and dropped a stun grenade. The guards jumped back, covering their eyes and ears. Drake jumped behind cover and exploded the next bombs, sending him flying out of the tent. He tried to get up and got shot at. The bullets ricocheted off the floor, but Drake rolled himself behind a low wall, saving himself. He returned fire and saw the guard get grabbed by a zombie, the two of them falling off the watch tower.

"Zombies … gotta … gotta love 'em." Drake laughed, catching his breath. He then looked up and was grabbed by a zombie. He yelled, pulling away and shooting at it, before getting swarmed by three more. Drake kicked them back and shot two before being thrown to the ground by the last one. He struggled, kicking it off and crushing its head. Drake coughed a bit and then saw a grenade roll by him. He jumped back, but the explosion caught him, sending him flying through an advertisement window, over the safety railings and through a small kiosk on the floor below. Everything was black for a few moments, and Drake rolled, almost passing out. His air had been forced out of him, and he almost passed out again. But he forced his way out of the broken kiosk, pushing wooden planks off of himself and crawling out of the rubble. He wasn't sure if he could walk after that one. Somebody then walked up and lifted him by the shirt. It was General Steel, the leader of the military expedition. He smirked and then punched Drake across the face and slammed him onto the floor. Drake choked, crawling very slowly away. Steel followed closely.

"You thought you could just come in here and blow my stuff up?" he asked, punting Drake in the ribs. Drake grunted, staggering to stand, and then turned sharply and punched Steel's face. Steel growled and caught his next punch, grabbing Drake and throwing him into a palm tree decoration. Drake didn't move much after that.

"You're nothing!" Steel screamed at him. "You've had too many little adventures, Drake, but you pissed in the wrong dog's yard. You don't get it, Drake—this is the cure. Burn Out. We kill everything in here, living or otherwise. To stop the infection—the 'zombies,' as you people have dubbed them. I've fought countless battles and won every one, and this is just another battle against the enemy."

Steel pulled out his gun and aimed at Drake, who was barely moving now. As a general, Steel's men had had a few encounters with Drake over the years. After all, this hadn't been Drake's first adventure, but the way things were looking, this might be his last.

"You are just another enemy," Steel said firmly.

A gun was fired. Drake closed his eyes and waited for moments, and then he looked to see Steel dropping to the ground, Sullivan standing behind him, his revolver still smoking.

"I never knew you were the kind to stay down, kid. Come on, get up," Sullivan said as he lifted Drake to his feet.

"Ugh, Sull … Sullivan?" Drake asked faintly, as his friend nodded. Drake smirked and laughed quietly; then he limped down the mall, using Sullivan to hold himself up before turning to see the burning military base.

"You really messed them up good," Sullivan complimented.

"Touché," Drake replied.

"Seriously, though, what were you thinking, Drake? Going up against the military? You can't keep being the lone hero!"

Sullivan berated him. Drake opened his mouth to talk back but was interrupted by a young girl.

"Excuse me, could you help us? We want a safe place to be, but Jimmy won't come," she pleaded. The two stared at each other and then followed her. She pointed at a closed store with several survivors in it. The girl then led them into the store and towards a flight of stairs leading down towards a locked door.

"See?" she said.

"All right, you stay here, we'll go check it out," Drake said, reassuring the girl before he and Sullivan walked down the stairs.

"Jimmy? You in there? You all right?" Drake called. No answer. Drake nodded, and Sullivan kicked in the door. The door led down to a basement. Drake and Sullivan went down and saw a strange sight. A young boy was scribbling furiously on the walls. When he turned his head, he had a crazed look on his face. Green goo was dripping from his mouth. The walls, roof, and floor were covered in markings, symbols, and pictures. All were made with green glowing ink. Sullivan looked down and there were empty vials scattered everywhere. He then pulled Drake's green vial from his vest.

"Thought you locked that up?" Sullivan asked with a grin.

"How did you ...? Never mind," Drake replied. Jimmy saw it and grabbed it fast, pouring most into his pen and the rest into his mouth.

"I hear the words. They're calling," Jimmy mumbled, finishing his picture and saying, "Drake Halberd ..." Drake felt his pouch heat up and pulled out the glowing green rock. It illuminated the wall, showing more green markings. But these were ones he could read. Drake's eyes grew, and then he quickly scraped the ink with a knife into a vial he'd grabbed off of the floor, getting as much goo as he could,

"Sullivan I have it, I have the cure. I know how to make it!"

CHAPTER 8: BITTEN

Drake placed the green goo in the compartment at the science lab, which he and the rest of the group had broken into after he and Sullivan returned from the military base. Using his knowledge of chemistry, he mixed his blood into the goo, creating a bluish green substance. The computer beeped twice and Drake rolled his chair over to it, typing as fast as he could. He was going on memory, but that had to be enough, because it was all he had. Drake took the vial and placed it inside a freezing system. Two minutes later, it was done. He removed it carefully and stared in amazement—the vial was full of blue glowing liquid. He rolled his chair over and pushed a button.

"Excuse me, guys, you can come in now," he said into the microphone. No one had been allowed in, so he could concentrate and remember what he had to do. The group— the twins, Mason, Sullivan, and Emma—all entered the room. They looked around and then saw the thing Drake was holding. Everyone rushed up to take a look, boosting Drake's prideful smile of accomplishment.

"What is it?" Jayde asked, shattering his daydream.

"It's the cure. I'm not sure how it works, but it should destroy the zombie virus," Drake replied. Mason took the vial, staring at it carefully as he rubbed his chin. He then pocketed the cure and pulled out his gun, shooting the machine that was producing more.

"Hey!" Jayde yelled standing up. Mason turned and shot her in the side.

"I'm sorry, sweetie, but one day you'll understand that what I have to do is necessary," he said with a hint of remorse. Angel ran over by Jade's side and Mason turned his gun towards Drake, who was reaching for a weapon. Sullivan grabbed a wood plank and smashed it down on Mason's arm. Sullivan swung again, but he was shot in the shoulder. Mason then ducked and ran as bullets whizzed by him. He escaped the room with Drake shooting the last of his bullets. Drake turned and went over to his friend.

"Sullivan!" he cried out. Sullivan coughed, smiled faintly, and spoke.

"Hey, kid, get him good, will ya?" Sullivan coughed more and lifted up his favourite revolver, passing it to Drake.

"Get him with this. It has only four bullets left, so make it count, eh." He breathed heavily again and shut his eyes. Emma ran over to Sullivan, shaking him.

"Take care of them Emma," Drake said, running out of the room. Drake ran fast, jumping over small stands and racing down the north wing, giving fast chase after Mason. Drake turned sharply, jumping onto a kiosk to avoid the grasp of some zombies, and then was forced down to avoid a few shots fired at him by Mason. Drake snarled and raised his gun, but he lowered it again, lacking a good shot. He continued the chase, until Mason turned and shot something above Drake. The chariot decor fell from the roof, and Drake jumped to the side, barely avoiding it. The chariot fell with a loud crack and crushed a few zombies that were charging Drake from the front, saving him. He stood up and then got raided by a pack of zombies that charged him from behind. Drake kicked a few back and shot one of them through the head. Drake then ripped out a plank from the destroyed chariot and beat the zombies with it. He turned to run but was grabbed and bitten in the forearm by a zombie. He screamed in pain and crushed the zombie's head and then turned to continue the chase. Drake checked out his arm. It was bad. He was bleeding, and it looked as if his wound had already started rotting, with his veins turning black as the infection spread. Sweat began to drip into his eyes, and he was totally winded. Drake slowed down and bashed through the door on his right, stumbling slightly as he worked his way through the north corridor. Drake then fell against a wall, catching his breath as his arm began to tingle and burn, as if it had fallen asleep. Forever. Drake shook it and then continued, determination the only thing keeping him standing. Drake kicked through the next door and was back into the mall. He looked around and then spotted a still fleeing Mason. Drake continued the chase, shooting at Mason and using his second shot, But Mason turned sharply, only getting grazed by the bullet. Drake cursed and then jumped onto the bench and vaulted over the high wall onto the second floor, rolling as he landed on his back with a thud. Drake sat up and pulled his way to his feet. The first thing he noticed was that he didn't feel pain, but his joints seemed stiffer. He then began to notice something else, the zombies were getting harder to see, as if they were fading away, but Mason, he was so much easier to spot now. Almost like a magnet pulling Drake towards him. That must've been why the zombies only attacked the living. Drake knew for sure now. He stood up and ran as fast as his weakening legs could go, but Mason was still far ahead. Mason shot again, this time missing. The bullet smashed into a massive ten-ton stand, destroying the support wires that held it up. Drake looked to his right and saw the stand falling fast. He jumped and it smashed through the floor, creating a hole too wide to avoid. Drake fell through three floors of the mall, smashing into several things along the way. He tumbled, and his hands grabbed at anything he could, but he fell into the darkness. Drake hit the ground with a thud, rolling onto his back and his hand slapped the ground. The last thing Drake saw before he blacked out was a strange woman running over and lifting him up.

Chapter 9: The Darkness

Drake opened his eyes, placing his hand over his forehead as he sat up, his head throbbing. As he shifted to an upright position, he thought of how often he had been knocked out the last day or so. Maybe none of this was real and he had brain damage? Drake shook his head and then heard a voice speak to him.

"You should be more careful. Don't move too fast." Drake looked and saw an Indian woman wearing loose clothes, a cloak resting on her shoulders. She was sitting across from him, and they were in what appeared to be a cave. She had long black hair and wore a silver piece of jewelry that had engraved lines crisscrossing each other, resting across her forehead.

Cave. The best word he could use to describe the place they were in. It was like a chamber in a massive ant nest, with a fire pit in the middle.

"Who … who are you?" Drake asked, shaking the cobwebs from his head. It was then that he noticed his arm. The skin was pale grey, and his veins were highlighted in black. Every one of them bulging out like it was a hot summer day, but black, as if he were a corpse. The woman across the room handed him a mirror, and he took note of his face—how a quarter of it, from his cheekbone to the middle of his forehead, was similar to his arm. And the rest of the veins on his face were beginning to turn.

"You don't have long," she said to him, stirring the fire.

"How am I still alive?" Drake asked, feeling his face.

"The only reason you're still alive is because of that stone, there, in your pocket," she answered. Drake looked down and pulled out the green glowing rock, staring at his lifeline.

"This thing never seems to break, and I've been through a lot with it." Drake chuckled slightly, placing his hand on his sore stomach and then putting the stone away. The woman looked at him grimly.

"Even with the stone, you don't have much time left. My name is Shyah. And this might seem strange, but I will tell you the cause of this outbreak. Deeper in these tunnels resides an ancient shrine that holds a jade mask, once blessed by the deities. However, seeking money and immortality, the man called Jax dug up this site to harvest the crystals raw energy so he could convert it into a potion. He built a mall over top to hide his discovery. In doing so, he defiled the mask and angered the deities, causing the dead to rise. Now the only way to stop it is for you to destroy the mask."

Drake stared at Shyah.

"There are zombies eating people, so that makes your story very believable at this point. But I have one question: why would Mason want the mask?"

"Power and greed. While wearing it, you can control them—the dead, that is—and become immortal yourself. Using a relentless horde, you could control the world."

"But why me? Why do I have to stop him? Everything I do I mess up. Now Sullivan could be dying, and all because I wanted a day off!"

"We don't choose our destinies, Drake Halberd. We can only choose to follow them or not."

Drake let his head hang low. He then rubbed his face with his hands. Having no other way out, he looked at Shyah and nodded.

"But how do I find my way out?" he asked.

"Let the light guide your way," Shyah replied before vanishing into the shadows. Drake shook his head and then turned and jogged off into a shadowy tunnel.

***

"Come on!" called a young girl's voice. Drake, nine years old, was following Serena to her secret hide out through a dark spelunker's cave.

"I'm trying, but it's too dark!" he whined, tripping over another rock. Serena turned around and stuck out her tongue.

"It's not too dark, silly. Just follow the light," she said cheerfully, cracking a green glow stick. Drake got up, wiping his eyes and followed her once more. Serena was his secret crush back then. And as a boy in love, he would follow her anywhere, no matter how stupid the idea was. She was about three months younger than him and had shoulder length blond hair and ice blue eyes. She wore a beige dress and danced through the cave elegantly.

"Come on!" she called again. This time her voice was followed by a rumble.

"What was that?" Drake asked fearfully. Serena looked around.

"Maybe it's a monster," she said in a ghostly voice, scaring Drake even more. "Come on! You said you used to survive on the streets, run from guards. How can this scare you?" she teased him. But that was different. Drake always had a phobia of caves and dark places. Adding in strange rumbles didn't help either. Drake shook his head and slapped his cheeks, looking as tough as possible for her. She smiled sweetly at him and then turned around. Another rumble came. Then another. Drake heard the loudest crack ever and the stones in the roof began to split and fall.

Earthquake.

Drake screamed for Serena, running as fast as he could. But time seemed to slow. A huge rock came crashing down, crushing the left half of her body and pinning her to the floor. More rocks crumbled, and everything grew darker. All Drake could see was Serena and her green glow stick illuminating the small space they were in. Drake cried a bit, crawling over to her and taking her hand. She stared at him, smiling faintly, trying to keep him as happy as she could. But he had seen through that "don't worry" smile. She was dying.

"Dr-ake?" she breathed out and he looked at her, tears covering his face.

"I was, taking you … here, to … give you something …" she started to say, taking pain wrenched breaths in between each word. She inched her hand over, passing Drake a small box. He opened it and in it was a small steel ring with beautifully etched markings and designs. A chain was looped through it so he could wear it as a necklace. Drake cried more and squeezed her hand tightly.

"So … when I was … gone, you could wear it, and keep me with you," she finished, still smiling that faint smile. Drake lowered his head. She knew that he was going to have to move away with Sullivan soon, so she had gotten him the ring so he would never forget her. She looked up and closed her eyes, breathing her last breath. Drake lay with her for what seemed like hours. Then he heard noises, and he heard the stones move. It was the towns folk, and with them was Sullivan, reaching his hand in for him. Drake took it and was pulled out, wearing her ring around his neck.

"Don't worry kid, I gotcha," Sullivan said as he picked Drake up. "So, where'd you get that nifty necklace?"

Drake squeezed the ring before answering.

"Serenity."

***

"Just follow the light."

He heard the words echo through his head. Drake pulled his rock from the pouch and it immediately illuminated his way through the tunnels. Drake ran ever faster down the lightened tunnel, until he passed through an archway. It led to a massive opening with a tall shrine. There were stairs leading up to the top, where an altar rested with nothing on it. Ascending those stairs, he saw Mason.

"Mason!" Drake screamed, catching his attention. Mason turned and smiled wickedly.

Chapter 10: The Key

The two exchanged glares as Drake clenched his fists. Mason turned and finished walking up to the altar.

"I was hoping you'd make it, Drake. Cause you always do. Don't you?"

"Mason, you destroyed this world's hope for a cure, you shot my friend and your own daughter! Was it really worth it?" Drake sneered back at Mason.

"This world needs a solid leader, one leader. All I want is a cure for this world. A cure for war. Peace. That's what I want. One day, I know my little girl will realize her sacrifice was for the greater good."

"Why didn't you just destroy the cure then?"

"This? This isn't the cure, you fool. This is the key. The key that gives way to immortality. You see, your blood, you were the key. That's why I had Jax start digging up the 'immortality juice.' The conspiracies, zombies, you just happening to be *here* in this very mall—it was all my doing you see. I knew you would have no choice but to be the hero. That's why I am here right now. It's all because of the both of us, and that's why it's you and me standing here, in this room. We are connected through fate."

"How do you know that?" Drake snarled back.

Mason's face then twisted into a wrinkled, psychotic smile.

"The mask told me," he stated with an evil laugh. Mason then turned towards the altar and continued, "You see, the mask, it speaks to me through my mind. Like the voice of the deities calling to me. I had heard about your exploits before, but had thought nothing of it. Then the deities told me that you were the key to freeing them and their powers. And that I had to be the one to do it, because I was destined to be immortal."

Mason placed the vial in a small hole at the centre of the altar, and the stones around Mason began to shift. They turned and rotated around, and the altar vanished under the walkway, giving way to a new shrine. One which held a jade mask that was glowing ever so slightly.

"Look at you, Drake," Mason said, "you're becoming one of them already. A zombie. You've had a good run, been useful, but you're done. You know it, why don't you join your friends in hell?"

Drake had heard enough and raced up the stairs, bull rushing Mason and tackling him to the ground. Mason growled and retaliated by head butting Drake in the face. Drake noticed how he had barely felt that and punched Mason across the face. Mason grabbed Drake, and they struggled for a bit before Mason was able to kick Drake off himself. Drake rolled around and got to his knees, trying to stand. Mason grabbed Drake from behind and wrapped his arm around Drake's neck, strangling him.

"Your legacy won't end with glory but with a sad little whimper," Mason mocked Drake.

Drake smiled and replied, "Don't grab a zombie—isn't that rule number one?" he said, before biting Mason in the forearm. Mason screamed and kicked Drake down the long row of stone stairs. Drake smashed into each step before reaching the bottom and rolling onto his back, moaning in agony. Mason shook off the pain in his arm and turned around, lifting the mask with both hands. He stared at it with lustful intent before lifting it towards his face.

Drake rolled onto his side and reached for his gun, Sullivan's gun, and aimed it as steadily as he could before firing it. The bullet traveled through the dusty air and into the back of Mason's head, hitting the mask on its way out. Mason dropped to his knees, falling off the shrine and into the abyss below. The jade mask hit the floor and bounced down the stairs, landing beside Drake's green stone. Drake watched as the two began to resonate with each other. They glowed brightly and sent pulses through the ground like a steady heartbeat. Drake grabbed his rock and with the rest of his strength lifted it high and smashed the mask into pieces. A bright green light burst out, exploding outwards like a massive shockwave, covering the entire mall. It then vanished, taking the mask and stone with it. Drake stood up slowly, staring at his hands. He was normal again. The zombie virus had been erased. Drake then looked towards the exit and limped his way out.

Everyone in the mall seemed to be cured. The zombie virus had been erased completely. No one seemed to remember what had transpired while they were infected.

EPILOGUE

Drake stood in a field of grass, staring at a stone in the ground with a name etched into it. Rain poured heavily down, soaking Drake from head to toe. But it didn't seem to bother him.

"I'm sorry, Drake, really," Emma said to him as she approached. "I know you two had been through a lot."

Drake nodded, and she leaned her head against him.

"How's Jayde?" he asked.

"She's doing just fine," said a voice from behind them. They turned to see Sullivan walking up to them, arm bandaged and in a sling.

"Sullivan," Drake said happily.

"Visiting Serena again?" Sullivan asked, and Drake nodded, looking back down at the tombstone.

As the rain began to clear, Drake looked up towards the sun, towards the light, and said, "Well, old man, where to next?"

"How about a vacation?"

"Are you kidding? That was my vacation. We've got more work to do, things to find, treasure to hunt!" Drake sneezed. Sullivan smiled and laughed.

"Sure, kid, sure."

Biography

D. J. Kowalenko was born and raised in rural Alberta. Second youngest of six children, he grew up playing video games and fighting for control of the TV remote. His wild imagination led him to write several stories, cumulating in his first published work, *Drake Halberd and the Veil of the Dead*.